P9-CRX-101

www.enchantedlion.com

First English-language edition published in 2021 by Enchanted Lion Books
248 Creamer Street, Suite 4, Brooklyn, NY 11231

Editors, English-language text: Claudia Zoe Bedrick and Emilie Robert Wong

A CIP is on record with the Library of Congress
ISBN 978-1-59270-373-9
Printed in Italy by Società Editoriale Grafiche AZ

First Printing

Betina Birkjær

Coffee Rabbit Snowdrop Lost

Illustrated by
Anna Margrethe Kjærgaard

Translated from Danish by
Sinéad Quirke Køngerskov

Enchanted Lion Books
NEW YORK

My grandfather's name is Kaj, and my grandmother's name is Gerda. I go to see them a lot.

My grandpa has 123 different flowers in his sunroom, and he knows the name of each one by heart. In Latin.

He calls me Stump.

Grandpa loves the smell of coffee, and Grandma loves crossword puzzles.

"An eight-letter word for the first sign of spring, starting with S," reads Grandma.

"*Galanthus nivalis*," answers Grandpa, while Grandma whispers "snowdrop" in my ear. Then I write "s n o w d r o p" with nice round letters.

"Well now, Stump. Isn't it about time you learned to drink coffee?" says Grandpa. I take a sip of my juice and answer with a burp, just a little one. Grandpa gives me a wink.

When Grandpa and I do jigsaw puzzles, we piece together the edge first. All four sides. Then we fill in the picture. We really like doing the one that has 1,000 pieces. It's a picture of a white rabbit in the snow.

Grandpa says that when I get a little older, I can have a rabbit. A little one. He had a little one when he was a kid, too.

"And it was called Stump, Stump," Grandpa says, with a wink. "That's the best name for little ones with long ears."

PUZZLE
1000

One day, Grandma reads, “A four-letter word for a fragrant flower with thorns.”

I already have the pencil in my hand, ready to write “r o s e,” but I wait for Grandpa to say the word. In Latin. Only this time, Grandpa can’t find the word.

Instead, he laughs and says, “Soon I won’t be able to remember my own name, either.”

“I’m sure it won’t come to that,” Grandma says, straightening her glasses.

I’m the only one who notices that Grandpa has lost something.

Rose

Autumn arrives,
and as the trees lose
more and more of their leaves,
Grandpa loses
more and more of his words.

Coffee

I collect all of Grandpa's lost words in a box.

It keeps me busy from morning to night.

Rabbit

One morning, Grandpa forgets the coffee cups.
He sets the table with wine glasses instead. The ones
that Grandma and Grandpa got as a wedding gift.

"We can't drink coffee from those," says Grandma.
She reaches for one, but it tips over and rolls off the table.
"For Pete's sake!" exclaims Grandma.

"Who is Pete?" asks Grandpa, looking at me.
But I don't know who Pete is, either.

Grandpa cuts himself when he tries to brush away
the shards of glass with his bare hands.

"Have you gone completely nuts?" says Grandma.
I go to get the bandages that Grandpa once bought for me.

When winter arrives, Grandpa seems to have lost all interest in doing anything. He just sits and stares out the window. Grandma thinks he's boring. She is looking for a five-letter word for a flower that starts with T.

"Can you get the rabbit for me?" Grandpa asks one day.
I take out the big jigsaw puzzle with the rabbit,
but Grandpa can't make sense of the 1,000 pieces.
Eventually, he pushes them onto the floor.
Grandma gets upset at the mess and goes to bed without
saying goodnight to Grandpa, even though she had
promised him she would never do that.

PUZZLE

While I clean up, Grandpa falls asleep on the couch. I pull the big blanket over him and take the little one for myself.

PUZZLE
1000

I wake up in the middle of the night. I'm freezing and all alone. I call for Grandpa, but only the cold answers me. A draft is coming from the sunroom, where the door is open. I wake up Grandma. The 123 flowers look like they haven't been tended to for a long time.

"Why didn't I notice this?" Grandma whispers, mostly to herself.

At first, we can see Grandpa's footprints in the snow, but before long, the wind blows them away. All the same, we can follow the words he's lost in the snow. Grandma can see them now, too.

House
Cold
Mittens
Snowdrop
Shoe
Snow

We spot Grandpa. He's sitting on a bench without a jacket, wearing only slippers on his bare feet. He mumbles something about not being able to find the rabbit. Grandma strokes his cheek.

"Who are you?" Grandpa asks, looking at me.

"It's me, Stump," I reply.

"Oh, I'm looking for my rabbit. It's lost," he sighs, blinking.

home
Stump
Gerda

When we get home, Grandma makes coffee and kisses Grandpa on the forehead. At first, Grandpa doesn't want the coffee, so Grandma holds the cup, with its spicy coffee scent, to his nose. Then he wants to drink it.

But mostly, Grandpa doesn't want to do anything anymore. He still likes to smell the flowers, but it's Grandma who takes care of them now. All 123 of them. Even though she doesn't know their names in Latin. My box of words is completely full.

"Let's have a party for Grandpa," I say to Grandma one day.

"What kind of party?" she asks.

"That kind of party," I say, pointing to their wedding picture.

"Just the three of us?" asks Grandma.

"The three of us and a surprise," I reply.

"A surprise?" she smiles.

"Just a little one," I say, with a wink.

PUZZLE
Flora
PHOTOS

I set the table with the nice glasses, and Grandpa decorates it with flowers. We have soup, a roast, and ice cream. Grandma takes out her wedding dress, and we put on some music. Grandpa hums along. We dance until we can't dance anymore.

"I just have to get something," I say, and I take out the box with the surprise.

“Well, well. What a lovely little one,” says Grandpa happily, lifting the rabbit out of the box.

It curls up on his lap and seems to like being scratched between its long ears.

“We can call it Stump,” I say. Grandma nods and says that’s the best name for little things with long ears. Grandpa smiles happily.

From that day on, my nickname is no longer Stump.

But I still have the box of Grandpa’s words. It will always remind me of how he—my grandpa—used to be.

Kai

Dementia and Memory

Ove Dahl, historian and head of the Danish Center for Reminiscence

When considering how people with dementia lose their memory, it's important to make the distinction between short-term and long-term memory. Often, as with Alzheimer's, it is primarily the short-term memory and cognitive skills that disappear in the initial, sometimes longer period of dementia. As is shown in this story, it could be knowing the Latin names of 123 different flowers, or knowing how to set the table for coffee that first goes. In contrast, and in many cases, a person retains their long-term memory with the onset of dementia, as when the grandfather forgets the present and goes out without a coat to look for the rabbit he remembers having as a child.

The word *reminiscence* is a recognized professional concept for planned and systematic work with human memories, such as within the field of dementia. It is about actively awakening and stimulating positive memories. This method can also help other people through difficult periods of their lives, such as children and adolescents with mental health problems, or migrants and refugees. For people with dementia, it is important to find the images, objects, songs, sounds, and smells that can bring back good memories and experiences. A good example of using the sense of smell is when the grandfather doesn't want coffee: "so Grandma holds the cup, with its spicy coffee scent, to his nose. Then he wants to drink it."

It is painful, but inevitable for relatives to accept that they can no longer be with the person with dementia in the same way as they were before. In other words, new ways of being together must be found so the person behind the dementia can be reached by stimulating their long-term memory. Stump finds a new way to reach Grandpa by planning to recreate his grandparents' wedding day, with decorations, food, clothes, music, and dancing. Experience also shows that children often find it easier to have natural relationships with frail older people than adults do.

Relatives know the life story of the person who has dementia and so quickly discover, through active reminiscence work, that objects can be a shortcut to the past. Rather than just talking about the past, it's about sensory and emotional experience as well. This occurs in the story for the grandfather when he touches the wedding dress and smells the coffee. Engaging with plants or flower scents would also have been stimulating possibilities for him. For those experiencing more severe dementia, who can no longer follow a short story or novel when read aloud, shorter texts, such as letters, postcards, poems, or even ticket stubs, programs, and advertisements, can be used. These can also give access to everyday life in the past in a concrete, immediate way.

When it comes to reminiscence, it doesn't matter whether the things talked about are true or not, because it's not about testing the person's ability to remember facts, like what year they got married. The important thing is to build good conversation and togetherness, to evoke recognition and joy in the present in the person with dementia. Such remembrance can also confirm who the person once was and still is. That said, the type of activities and materials that are useful and suitable for an individual must be continuously assessed.

As dementia progresses, the person loses more and more ways to express themselves and communicate. Here, relatives need to further develop and strengthen their communication in parallel. If the person is bedridden, one can, for example, place familiar items on a shelf or hang them on the wall—things that evoke fond memories. Working with reminiscence can, in some ways, be compared to detective work, where the people closest to the person with dementia do the work to reveal and evoke good memories.

In addition to the pictures and objects in the home of the person with dementia, other items connected to the person's youth can be found at flea markets or online. You can also find information at the Dementia Society of America, which focuses on enhancing life, providing materials and resources, and recognizing and encouraging all those who provide dementia care (www.dementiasociety.org).